Cosmo and the Robot

BRIAN PINKNEY

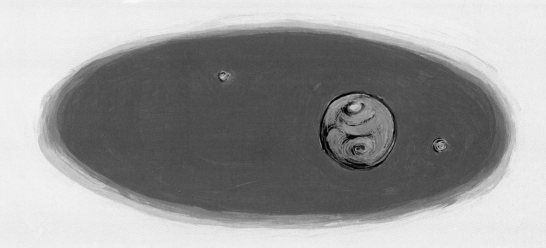

GREENWILLOW BOOKS • *An Imprint of HarperCollinsPublishers*

To Dobbin, my little explorer

Scratchboard, Luma dyes, and acrylic paints were used for the full-color art.
The text type is Avant Garde Medium BT.

Cosmo and the Robot
Copyright © 2000 by Brian Pinkney
Printed in Singapore by Tien Wah Press. All rights reserved.
http://www.harperchildrens.com

Library of Congress Cataloging-in-Publication Data

Pinkney, J. Brian.
Cosmo and the robot / by Brian Pinkney.
    p.   cm.
"Greenwillow Books."
Summary: Cosmo, a boy living on Mars, must come up with a quick solution
when his malfunctioning robot Rex threatens his sister, Jewel.
ISBN 0-688-15940-0 (trade).   ISBN 0-688-15941-9 (lib. bdg.)
[1. Robots—Fiction.   2. Mars (Planet)—Fiction.   3. Science fiction.]   I. Title.
PZ7.P63347Co   2000   [E]—dc21   98-32209   CIP   AC

1 2 3 4 5 6 7 8 9 10   First Edition

Rex was Cosmo's best friend.

Rex was a gentle robot,
afraid of his own shadow, and
Cosmo liked him that way.

Rex was not like Cosmo's big sister, Jewel,
who bossed him around.

But one day Rex bumped his head and started acting
like a monster. Cosmo's mother examined Rex and
told Cosmo that Rex was broken for good.
So Cosmo's father hauled Rex to the asteroid dump.
"It's for the best," said his mother.
"So long, clunker," said Jewel.
But Cosmo was sad.
He knew that life on Mars
would never be the same.

To cheer him up, Cosmo's parents gave Cosmo a
Super Solar System Utility Belt with ten supersonic attachments.
Cosmo took apart Jewel's Easy Bake oven with the
Saturn Ring Screwdriver.
"You're a pain, comet-head!" yelled Jewel.
"Give me back my Saturn Ring Screwdriver," said Cosmo.

"Kids, please," said Cosmo's mother.

"I can't hear myself think!" exclaimed Cosmo's father.

So Cosmo and Jewel were sent to Zone 5 to collect rocks for an alpha-proton experiment.

"I don't want any dilly-dallying," warned their mother.

"And Jewel, you keep an eye on Cosmo," said their father.

"Collecting rocks is so boring," said Jewel. "I don't know why we had to come to this stupid planet anyway. Do you have to bring that dumb belt with you everywhere you go?"

"I don't know," said Cosmo.

Cosmo and Jewel came across
an abandoned terrain rover.
Cosmo started taking it apart with his
Mercury Magneto Wrench.

"Come on, space-cadet, let's go. Do you have to play with junk all the time?" asked Jewel.

"I don't know," said Cosmo.

He saved the nuts and bolts in his Neptune Specimen Bag.

"Look, I can't take this baby-sitting stuff.
I know where the best rocks are," said Jewel.
"You wait here and I'll be back in a little while."
Cosmo examined the sockets and caps
with his Uranus Ultra-Magnifying Glass.

Cosmo finished pulling apart the terrain rover.
But Jewel did not come back,
and it would be dark soon.

After a while Cosmo took out
his Pluto Maxi-Scope Binoculars
to look for Jewel.

When Cosmo zoomed in,
he saw Jewel in the asteroid dump
running from a big, scary robot.

IT WAS REX!

Cosmo raced to the dump,
crouched near a boulder,
and checked his gear.
He could hear Jewel yelling,
"Leave me alone!
You big metal-mouth!"

Cosmo called Rex on his Venus Antenna-Speaker Phone.

"Rex! Stop! It's me, Cosmo, your friend."

But Rex didn't stop.

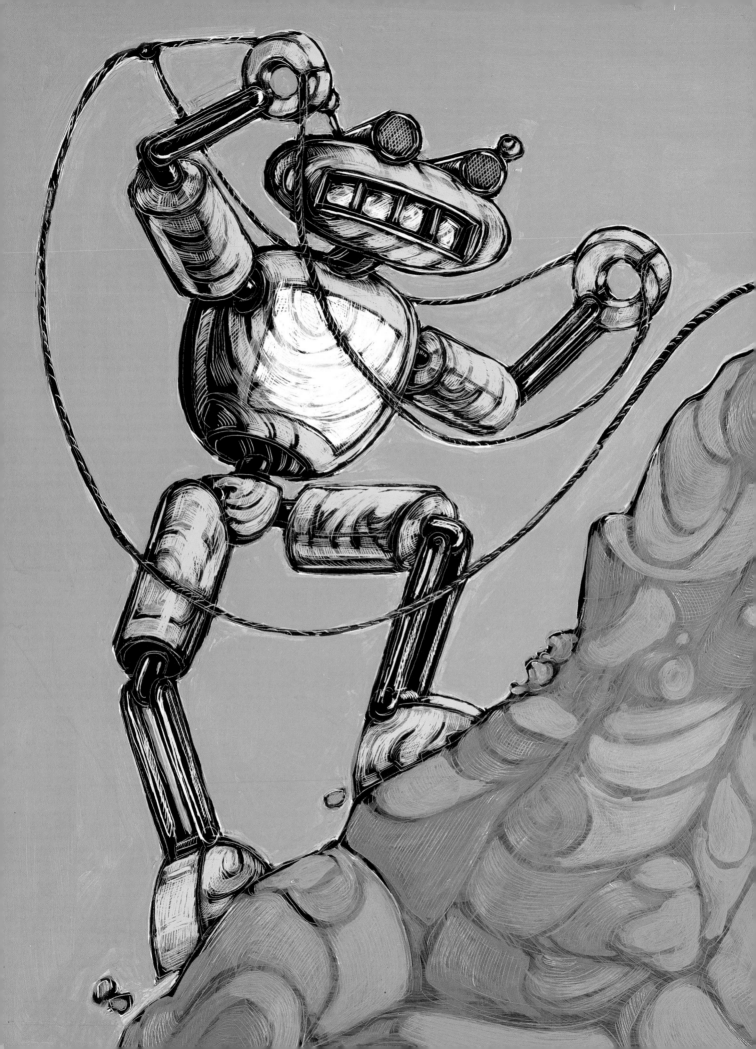

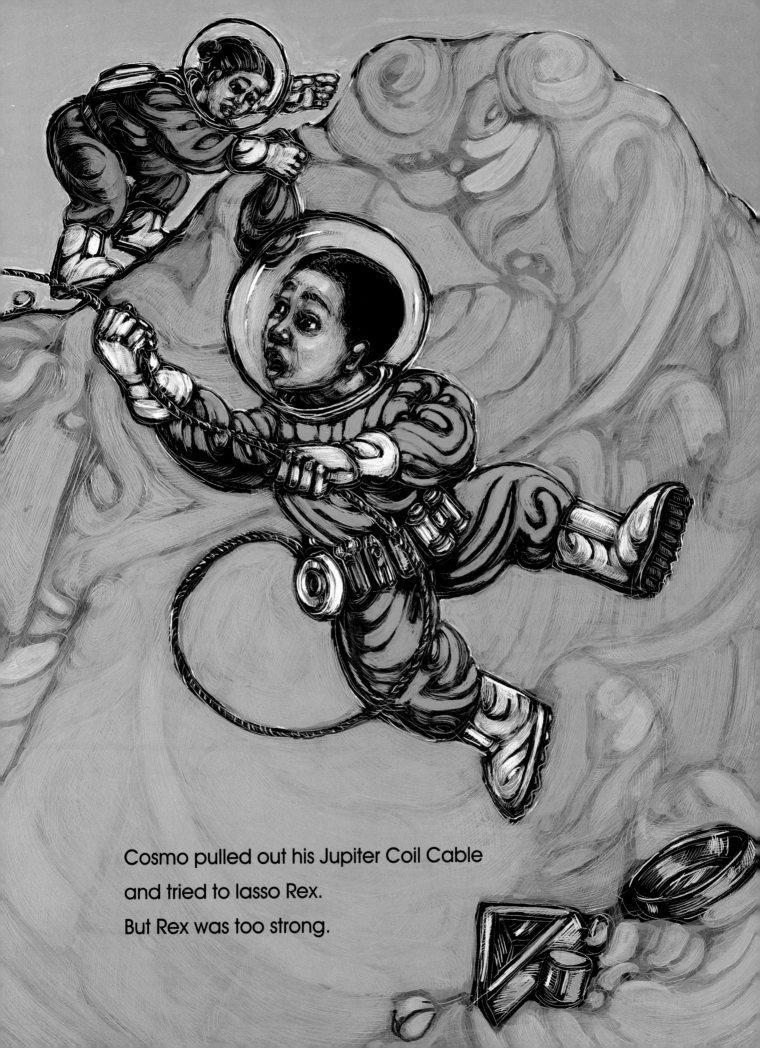

Cosmo pulled out his Jupiter Coil Cable
and tried to lasso Rex.
But Rex was too strong.

Just as Rex lunged for Jewel, Cosmo made
a huge dinosaur head, using his hand and
his Sun Laser-Beam Flashlight. A scary shadow!
Rex started to tremble.
He stepped backward
and fell.

KABOOM!

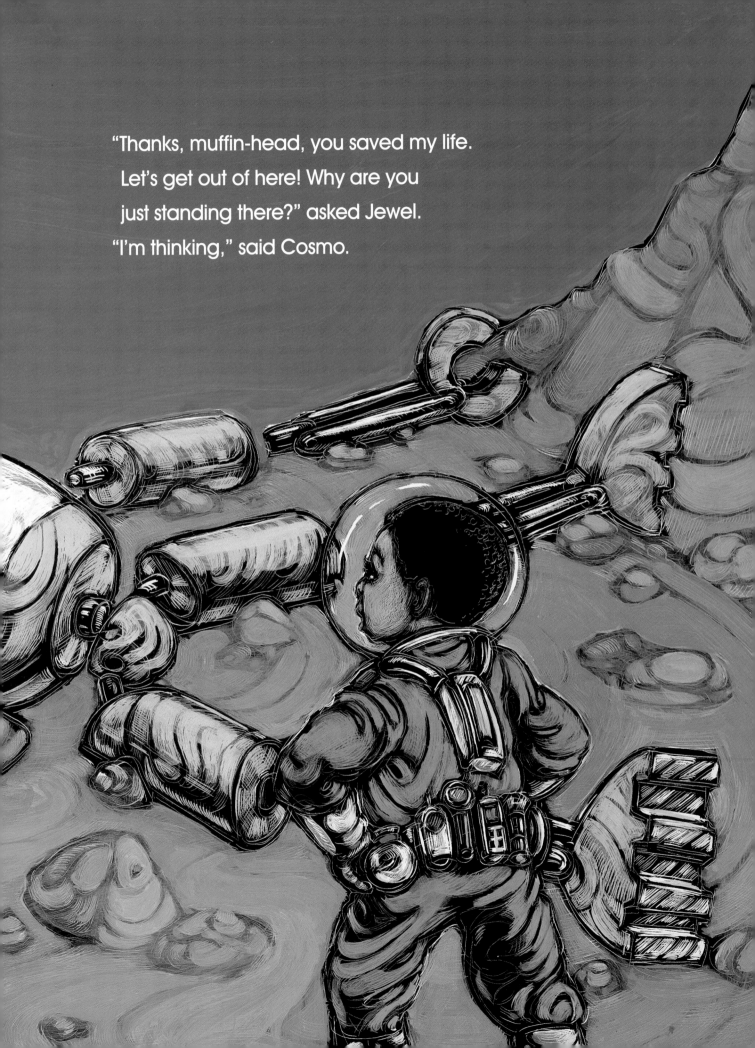

"Thanks, muffin-head, you saved my life.
Let's get out of here! Why are you
just standing there?" asked Jewel.
"I'm thinking," said Cosmo.

"Don't touch that.
   What are you doing?" asked Jewel.
"I'm fixing Rex," said Cosmo.

"Cut that out. That
looks dangerous.
Do you know what
you're doing?"
asked Jewel.
"I think so,"
said Cosmo.

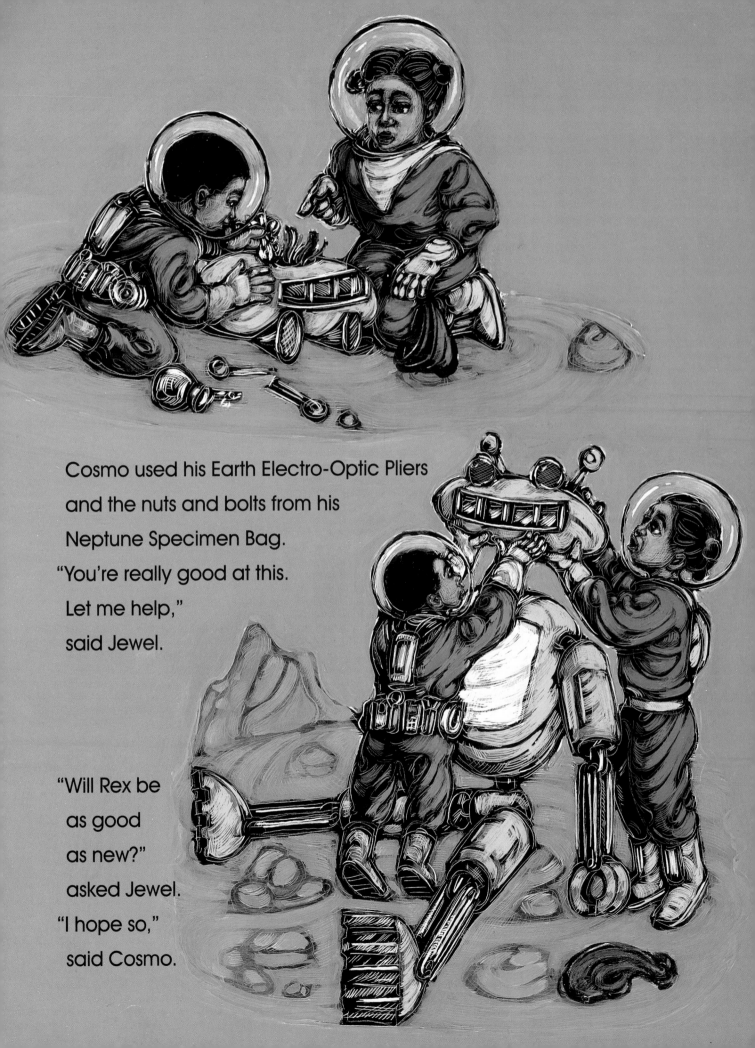

Cosmo used his Earth Electro-Optic Pliers
and the nuts and bolts from his
Neptune Specimen Bag.
"You're really good at this.
Let me help,"
said Jewel.

"Will Rex be
as good
as new?"
asked Jewel.
"I hope so,"
said Cosmo.

When Rex stood up and put Cosmo on his back,
Cosmo was so happy he let Jewel hold his
Mars Micro-Radar Homing Device.
Cosmo, Jewel, and Rex headed for home,
collecting rocks as they went.

"Wait until Mom and Dad see Rex. I'm going to tell them how you fixed him. When we get home, will you fix my Easy Bake oven?" asked Jewel.
"Sure," said Cosmo.

And Cosmo knew
that life on Mars
would be better than ever.

SUPER SOLAR SYSTEM UTILITY BELT with supersonic attachments

TEN STATE-OF-THE-ART FEATURES INCLUDE:

Sun Laser-Beam Flashlight This is the light to keep on hand. Provides full-spectrum extra-intensity light with electro-luminescent bulb.

Mercury Magneto Wrench Get a grip! This amazing high-tech tool comes with built-in magnetic sensory handle.

Venus Antenna-Speaker Phone Keep in touch with a friend. Easy-to-use duplex voice-activated transmission and signal amplifier.

Earth Electro-Optic Pliers It's that simple. Incredible precision self-adjusting wire locator and cutter.

Mars Micro-Radar Homing Device Find your way home from any Zone with combined maximum-long-range transmitter and auto scan.

Jupiter Coil Cable Hold on tight! Includes mega-strength high-speed retractor and swivel belt clip.

Saturn Ring Screwdriver Give it a twist. Complete with anti-slip rotation ring for precise performance.

Uranus Ultra-Magnifying Glass Too small for the naked eye? Not any more, with five atomic digital magnification settings.

Neptune Specimen Bag You'll have no more lost nuts and bolts with four multi-capacity storage compartments.

Pluto Maxi-Scope Binoculars Take a look. Advanced mini-optics lets you see day or night with dual-action auto-focus and power zoom.

RECHARGEABLE BATTERIES NOT INCLUDED